My Mom is Beautiful

by: Jamie Lynn Anhalt

My mom is beautiful.
She is not like the rest.

strongly be...
moment you decia...
...er at your chosen
...e, you'll become m...
...e to learn. My jo...

She soars
above everyone.
She is truly the
best.

She liked to dance and sing.
Even sometimes on a chair.

She
shopped
'til she
dropped.
Her style
really had
flare.

She was the best friend to have because she always cared.

She loved my dad with all her heart because he always had ice cream to ♥ share.

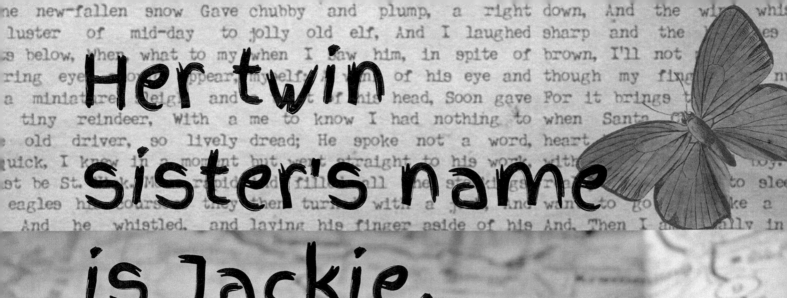

Her twin
sister's name
is Jackie.

They look exactly
the same.

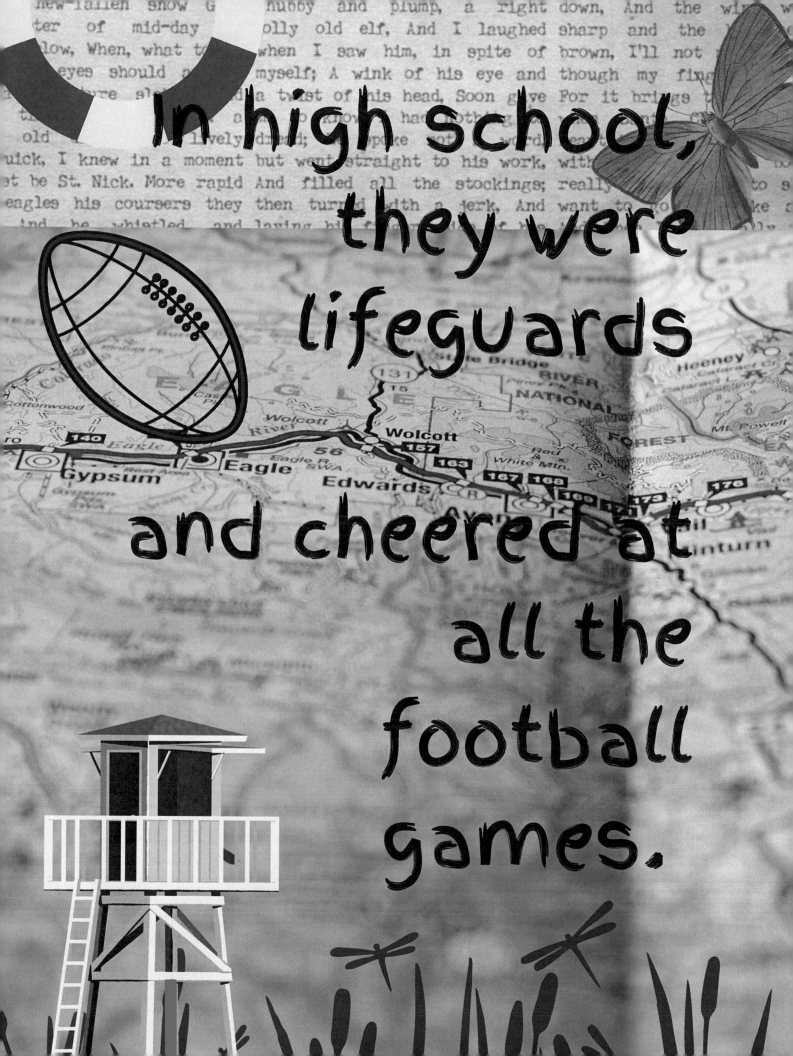

In high school, they were lifeguards and cheered at all the football games.

She sometimes got tired, but that was okay.

She was a warrior, a scientist, and a patient. She was strong all day.

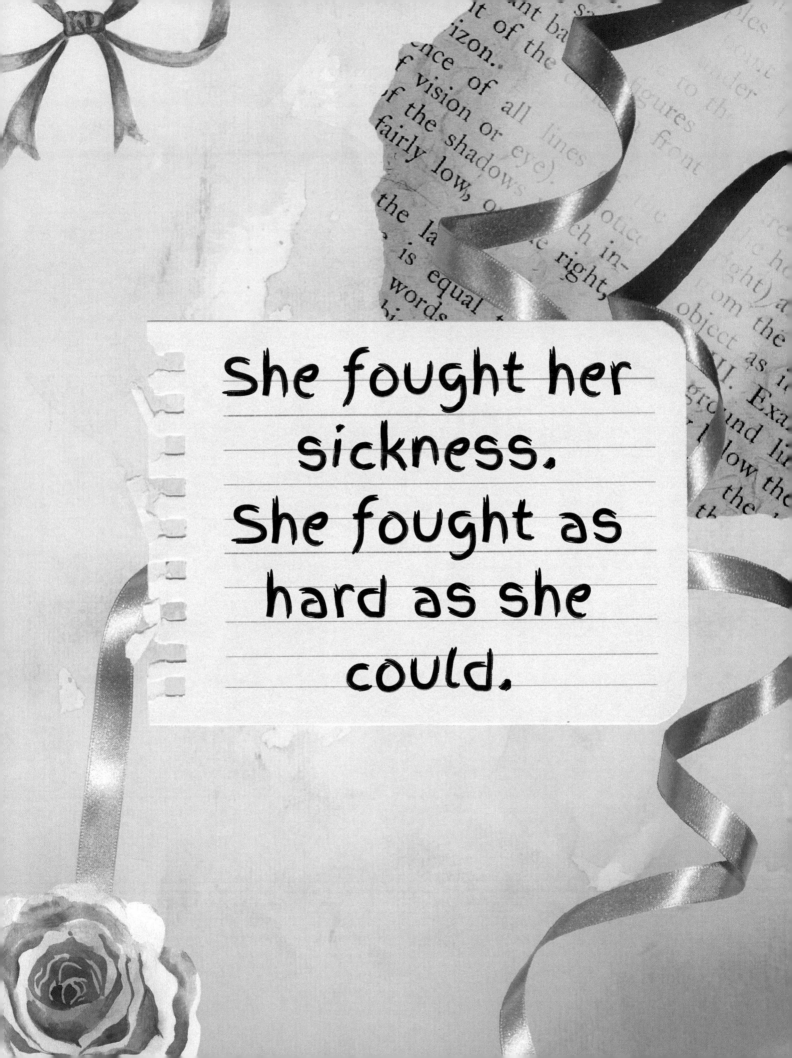

It was time to
tell her goodbye.

A day no one
thought would
come.

A daughter without her mother.

I thought "what will I become?"

We all needed a little bit of help. Especially from good friends like Natalie.

xo, Natalie

It's okay that
I cry
sometimes
still,
I also laugh
and smile

When I think of fun times like walking on the beach for miles.

All our moms look different. They come in many forms.

But no matter what they will comfort you through any storm.

I miss my mom. I really wish she was still here,

but I think of her often so my favorite memories never fail to appear

My mom is beautiful. I am sure yours is too.

So give her an extra hug tonight and never forget to say "I love you."

Denise (Christie) Anhalt lost her courageous battle with breast cancer Thursday, May 9, 2019. Denise was born in Philadelphia, and grew up in Langhorne, graduating from Bishop Conwell High School in 1983. She earned her Bachelor of Science degree in Nursing from the University of Scranton in 1987. She worked as a nurse for a long while, but then furthered her career at Bristol Myers Squibb as the Head of Clinical Operations in Innovative Medicines. Besides work, Denise enjoyed spending time with family and friends, watching her children compete in sports, and relaxing at the Jersey shore, especially Cape May, N.J. She also loved listening to country music and attending concerts. She is missed by her family, friends, and coworkers everyday.

Made in United States
North Haven, CT
26 October 2022